HOLLY HOBBIE

A Cat Named Swan

Random House New York

Copyright © 2017 by Holly Hobbie

All rights reserved. Published in the United States by Random House Children's Books,
a division of Penguin Random House LLC, New York.

Random House and the colophon are registered trademarks
of Penguin Random House LLC.

Visit us on the Web! randomhousekids.com

Educators and librarians, for a variety of teaching tools,
visit us at RHTeachersLibrarians.com

Library of Congress Cataloging-in-Publication Data is available upon request.
ISBN 978-0-553-53744-4 (trade) — ISBN 978-0-553-53745-1 (lib. bdg.) — ISBN 978-0-553-53746-8 (ebook)

Book design by Martha Rago

MANUFACTURED IN CHINA
10 9 8 7 6 5 4 3 2 1
First Edition

For the Vermonters:
J.T., H.H., N.H., and Q.T.H.

—H.H.

Then he was alone. Where was his mother?
What had happened to his brothers and sisters?
They were gone.

The streets were a place
of constant danger.

Yet day by day, he found enough food to eat.
Day by day, he managed to elude the threats
that surrounded him. He survived.

One morning, though, he did not escape the
peril that came down on him.

But now there was food. Soon, when nothing harmed him or frightened him, he became less afraid. The new place was safe. Boredom was better than misery.

Then the boredom ended. He was swept up. There were voices and laughter. There was motion and sunshine and blue sky. He was swept away.

Day by day, he learned about his new surroundings.
He learned about the people there, their comings
and goings, their voices and their touch. He learned
the name they gave him: Swan. He learned about the
dog, its bark and bluster. Day by day, he learned about
being here.

After many days had passed, he learned that the house was his house, the yard was his yard. He learned that the people were his people and he was theirs. He belonged to them and they belonged to him. After many days had passed, he knew that the days would continue to come and go in the same way.

Allison gave him breakfast in the kitchen before anyone else was up.

"Good morning, Swan. How are you today? Oh, what a nice boy you are. What a pretty boy."

After breakfast, he bounded into the outdoors, if it wasn't raining or snowing, to make his usual rounds of the stone wall, the apple tree, and the garden. Bumblebees made him buzz with excitement, and butterflies made him soar.

He had several places for his morning nap. A patch of sun in the midst of Allison's houseplants was perfect. Sometimes he went upstairs to Molly's bed. Or he would doze in Allison's studio while she was working at her drawing table.

"Hello, Swan. Is it time for your nap? What a sleepy boy."

After lunch, he plunged into the outdoors again to hunt along the lilac hedge or chase leaves in the backyard or nimbly scramble up the towering maple tree. Birds cast a spell. Woody was almost always outside, and provoking Woody led to big barking excitement.

If it was a warm day, he would take his afternoon nap under the low branches of the evergreen at the edge of the garden.

Everyone returned home at the end of the day like a surprise.

"Hi, Swannie," said Molly. "What have you been doing all day?"

"There you are," said Bill. "Have you been taking good care of Allison?"

"Does Swansie want Willy to pet him?" said Willy. "Oh, that feels good. What a lazy Swansie."

Molly usually gave him his evening meal.

"Who's going to get fat?" Molly said. "Who's getting a big belly?"

He liked to lie under the table, listening, while the family had their dinner.

He spent part of each evening thoroughly grooming himself.

"Aren't those paws clean?" Allison said. "They must be clean by now."

Later he went to the living room to pick a lap to lie on. And there were plenty of places to sleep at night. There was his own bed in the kitchen, but there was also the couch in the living room, or the folded blanket on the chair by the fireplace.

But Swan's very favorite place to sleep
was in Molly's bed, all curled up right next
to Molly on her perfectly soft blanket.

"What a beautiful boy," whispered Molly.
"What a lovely Swan."

Each day now was like that. Each day was perfect.